AuthorHouse™
1663 Liberty Drive
Bloomington, IN 47403
www.authorhouse.com
Phone: 833-262-8899

Because of the dynamic nature of the Internet, any web addresses or links contained in this book may have changed since publication and may no longer be valid. The views expressed in this work are solely those of the author and do not necessarily reflect the views of the publisher, and the publisher hereby disclaims any responsibility for them.

This book is printed on acid-free paper.

ISBN: 978-1-7283-0823-4 (sc)
ISBN: 978-1-7283-0824-1 (e)

Print information available on the last page.

Published by AuthorHouse 12/03/2020

authorHOUSE®

A MONKEY'S TALE OF TRAVEL AND TIES

BOOK # 1

Written & created by: Sandra Z. Katchuk, RN OBGYN

From

Grammy's Sandbox Collection of

Stitches in Rhyme-Story time books and quilts

Revised December 2016, 2020

Dedicated to all my children
and
Parents everywhere

They who pray/play together

Stay together

Designs by Dakota Collectibles

"A Monkey's Tale of Travel & Ties"

No matter where life's dreams lead you to ramble & roam

Never forget, your family awaits to welcome you home

"I'm tired of this silly ol' Jungle," Morgan Monkey sighed. "I wanna explore someplace new–

But, where shall I go? I haven't a clue."

"It's boring hanging upside down by my tail in mid-air"

"And, swinging on vines through the trees-gives me quite a scare!"

"Guess I"ll just sit here and eat my banana stew,

Until I can tell this jungle life, toodle-oo."

"I can beat my drums to call the King for advise,

He'll tell me where to find an exciting new paradise."

"Good day Tiger King Kyle."

"Please kind Sir, do you know of new scenery away from this zoo,

For a lil' monkey to see, or things that a lil' monkey can do?"

"Indeed!" roared Tiger King Kyle.

"You can visit the South Carolina ocean and play in the sand."

"Ooh that sounds nice," smiled Morgan Monkey. "But, which way do I go to find such a land?"

"I'll ask Parker Parrot, the Jungle Park Ranger.

"Pardon me Mr. Parker-

Can you tell me how I'm to reach

The Great Swamp City, of seashells and sandy beach?"

"Easy-Breezy," Parker Parrot replied. "Just relax at the Hotel Hammock

And, let only happy thoughts fill your head as you gently rock."

"Then like the butterflies fluttering in the air,

Your mind will take wing, and soon you'll be there."

"Well imagine that clever scheme,

I can go anywhere I choose,

I need only to dream."

Suddenly Lydia Lioness, the jungle guardian of all, did appear-

"Well lil' monkey, it seems you're ready to travel far, far away from here."

"My prayers will keep you from harms-way

Until you return to us at the end of your stay."

Morgan Monkey yawned, "I do thank you, Queen Lydie,

Good-bye now, I'm off to visit the Walterboro City."

"Hey, Mr. Levi Elephant, if you please-

Will you help me prepare for my day dream search for the Palmetto Breeze?"

"Certainly," Levi Elephant grinned,

"I'll spray you down with my long hose nose.

You'll be squeaky clean from your lil' monkey head to your lil' monkey toes."

"Howdy-do, Miss Jena Giraffe, may I beg from you a ride?

I must find the ACE Basin door and seashore, before noon's high-tide."

"Sure, hop aboard my back,"

Jena Giraffe agreed.

"I'll have you there licka-de-split, just let me lead."

"Sweet!" squealed Morgan Monkey.

"Pretending is really neat."

First I was a famous surfer, who caught the perfect wave.

And, I raced down a tall water slide- goodness, I'm so very brave!

Then I became a great deep sea diver-
Exploring for treasures beneath the salty water.

I went on a camp out, and had the best Banana roast

On a Low Country Plantation, where folks are a grand southern host.

Next, I took a bike ride along the Wildlife nature trail.

I had to pedal faster & faster so Wally, the Gator, couldn't chomp off my tail!

Swamp
Gators

CHOMP CHOMP!

I played at a friendly bowling alley in the city's historic Hickory Valley.

Bowling for bananas was so much fun

1-2-3 strikes, and "I won!"

I even stopped at Dairy Land for a huge
Banana Split,

Yum! I ate and ate, 'til I could barely move or sit.

Taking a banana boat tour, now came to mind-

So much to do here, so little time.

But, I paddled the Chessey Creek for a mile-

What an exciting journey I've had, sure makes one smile.

Alas, my make-believe venture must come to an end.

I really missed Brycie Baboon- my very best friend.

Brycie 'Boon cried, "Yea! You've come back to our jungle den."

"Are you ready to play our favorite games again-

Of hide n' seek and peek-a-boo

Among the jungle flowers and the tall bamboo?"

"You bet!" chimed Morgan Monkey.

"But, my next jungle escape you must all come too,

For we're a family and families stick together like glue."

Now it's time for Jungle kids to jump into your nest.

But before lil' sleepy heads are laid to rest-

Give thanks to God for day dreams of delight

And, to keep y'all safe 'til the new morning's light.

Sweet dreams my little

Coconuts and Goodnight!

May God Bless you always—sleep tight.

All my Love,

Grammy

From your home to mine-

We'll find two paths, to which the

road does wind

Faithfully, we'll also find the extra

needed time

For without you, your family will

always pine.

The end

of my

tale

K

nted in the United States
Bookmasters